TOWSER
and the Water Rats
Tony Ross

Andersen Press · London
Hutchinson of Australia

© 1984 by Tony Ross. First published in Great Britain in 1984 by Andersen Press Ltd.,
19–21 Conway Street, London W.1. Published in Australia by
Hutchinson Group (Australia) Pty. Ltd., Richmond, Victoria 3121.
All rights reserved. Printed in Great Britain by
W.S. Cowell Ltd., Ipswich

ISBN 0 86264 051 2

Sometimes, at weekends in the summer, Towser liked to go to his holiday house by the water. He enjoyed everything about his holiday; he enjoyed packing his things, he enjoyed the bus trip to the river, but most of all, he enjoyed. . .

...just lazing about, doing *nothing much*.

He liked to fish. He never caught anything, but then he never wanted to. It was just nice to lie, watching his float, nodding "Howdyedos" to the dragonflies, and generally enjoying the doingnothingmuchedness of it all.

Nothing much ever happened on the river, except on the one day that the Water Rats arrived.

The Water Rats owned a steamer, so they started a shipping company and did small nautical jobs for the animals who lived near the river.

Towser thought that the Water Rats were noisy scallywags.

As the Water Rats neared Towser's summer house,
Cap'n Rat spied out the land with his spy-glass.

"Hmmmm!" he muttered. "Dumby dumdy dum, that
looks just about right. Hard over, bring her round,
make for that summer house over there. *Steeeeeeady!*"

The Water Rats landed, after much bumping and splashing.

"Good day, sir," said the Cap'n. "We couldn't help noticing your fine summer house."

Towser opened one eye.

"It's well built, and in just the right place to be the head office of our shipping company."

Towser opened the other eye.

Towser didn't say anything. He just watched as the rats examined the summer house.

They pushed it, to see if it would fall over.

They poked it, to see if the wood was rotten.

They looked at the bottom, to see if it was firmly fastened to the ground.

All the time, they chattered and squeaked with excitement.

They even climbed on to the roof, to look for leaks.

At last, Cap'n Rat spoke. "We'll give you *two* pence for it," he said. "We've looked at it carefully, and it's worth no more."

"Worth no more!" squeaked the other rat, who seemed to do all the work.

Towser frowned.

"I don't really want to move," said Towser. "I like it here, it's nice."

"*Three* pence then!" snapped Cap'n Rat.

Towser showed the Water Rats the inside of the summer house. "Look how cosy it is. The television works. It's worth more than three pence."

"*Four* then!" growled the Cap'n. "And that's me last offer."

"Done!" said Towser. "On one condition."

"I want *one* ride on your steamer."

"*Done!*" grinned Cap'n Rat, and paws were shaken.

Towser put his four pence in a safe place. Then he began to load *all* his furniture and things on to the little steamer.

"*Hey!* What d'ye think you're *doing*?" screeched the Cap'n.

"I'll take my ride *now*," answered Towser.

"How long is it going to take then?" moaned the Cap'n.

"Oh, I don't know," yawned Towser, making himself comfy. "It depends how much I like it. Maybe all summer."

The two rats quivered with rage. "We've got a living to make!" they screamed. "And you're taking up most of our boat."

Then Towser had another of his ideas. "Tell you what," he said.

"I'll buy back that summer house. I'll give you *two* pence for it."

"But we gave you *four*," wailed the Cap'n.

"You both said it was only worth *two*," pointed out Towser.

The rats had no answer to that, so they had to accept Towser's offer.

Two pence were handed over.

"Better put my things back in my house then," said
Towser, and the rats were only too happy to oblige.
They arranged the furniture neatly again, before
Towser changed his mind. Then they jumped back in
their steamer and set off down river, as Towser counted
his two pence profit.

Towser watched the little steamer puff its way about its business. He stood outside his house and sniffed the air. It was a perfect evening.

"I'm glad things turned out like that..." he said, to nobody in particular,

"*...I hate boats!*"

British Library Cataloguing in Publication Data
Ross, Tony
  Towser and the water rats.
  I. Title
  823'.914[J]   PZ7

ISBN 0-86264-051-2